This Topsy and Tim book belongs to

_____

This title was previously published as part of the *Topsy and Tim Learnabout* series
Published by Ladybird Books Ltd
80 Strand London WC2R ORL
A Penguin Company

5 7 9 10 8 6

ISBN-13: 978-1-90435-129-0
ISBN-10: 1-90435-129-8

Printed in Italy

Go to the Doctor

Jean and **Gareth Adamson**

It was a cold and misty morning.
Mummy cooked a tasty hot breakfast
for Topsy and Tim.
"Don't want any breakfast," said Tim.

"Oh, you are a misery,"
said Mummy crossly.
Dad was not cross, but then he
had not cooked the breakfast.
"This isn't like Tim," he said.
"There must be something wrong.
Open your mouth wide, Tim."
Tim's throat was swollen and red.
"Poor old Tim," said Dad.

Mummy phoned the Health Centre.
She made an appointment for Tim
to see Dr Sims.
They walked to the Health Centre.
Tim wore his scarf up over his nose
to keep his sore throat warm.

HEALTH CENTRE

The receptionist checked Tim's
appointment in her big book.
She told them to go and wait
outside Dr Sims' surgery.
"Look," said Topsy. "There's Kerry."
Kerry was one of Topsy and Tim's
school friends.

"What's the matter, Kerry?"
asked Topsy.
"It hurts when I swallow,"
Kerry said.
"Tim has a sore throat too,"
said Topsy.
Tim just looked glum.

Soon it was Tim's turn to go into
the surgery.
"Good morning," said Dr Sims.
"Good morning, Dr Sims," said Topsy.
Tim said nothing.

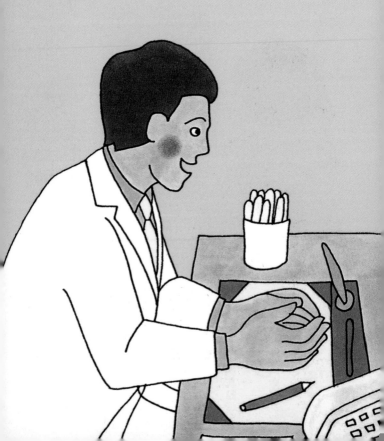

"Tim isn't talking," Topsy explained.
"I think it's because his throat hurts."

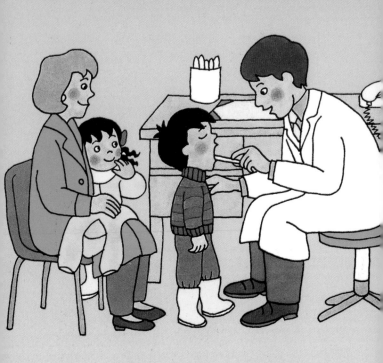

"Open your mouth, Tim,"
said Dr Sims, "and let me see."
Dr Sims took a little flat stick
and held it on Tim's tongue.
"Say ah," he said.

Then he looked at Tim's eyes
and inside his ears.
"You must have bad ear-ache too,
Tim," he said.
Tim nodded.
"You're a brave lad," said Dr Sims.

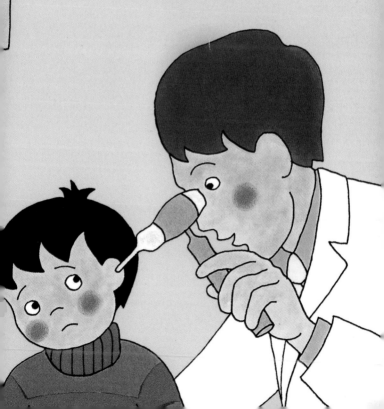

"Mmm," said Dr Sims. "Up with your
jumper, young man."
He put his stethoscope into his ears
and listened to Tim's chest.

"That looks like a telephone," said Tim.
"Yes," said Dr Sims. "I can hear what
chests and tummies are saying through
it. The sound tells me if people are ill."
Then he let Topsy listen to Tim's heart.

Dr Sims wrote a prescription and gave
it to Mummy.

"One spoonful four times a day," he
said. "This will soon make you feel
better, Tim."

Mrs White, the pharmacist, prepared Tim's medicine and gave it to Mummy. "Make sure he takes all the medicine," she said.

Mummy put the medicine safely
in her bag.
Just then, Kerry came past.
"I've got some medicine," she said.
"Tim's got some too," said Topsy.

When they got home, Mummy took out the medicine. It had a special childproof top, but Mummy could open it. She poured out a spoonful for Tim. "Did it taste nice?" asked Topsy. "Mmm," said Tim, licking his lips.

Then Mummy locked the bottle of
medicine away in a cupboard, out
of Topsy and Tim's reach.

When Dad came home, Tim was
tucking into blackcurrant jelly.
Topsy was not eating hers.
"She's sulking because she
isn't ill," said Tim.
"I wonder," said Dad. "Open wide,
Topsy, and let Dr Dad have a look."
Topsy's throat was red and sore.

Dad took Topsy to the Health Centre that evening. Her throat was sore but she was proud to be going to see the doctor.

Dr Sims was not there, so Topsy saw
Dr Jaunty instead. She came home
with a bottle of medicine just like Tim's.